**Sheila Mary Taylor** was born in Cape Town of Scottish immigrants, Dr James Garden Taylor, psychologist, behavioural scientist and author; and Dora Taylor, novelist, poet, playwright and literary critic. Sheila studied at the Cape Technical College, and also trained at the University of Cape Town Ballet School after which she went to the UK to further her career as a dancer. Instead she met and married Colin Belshaw, a mining engineer. The couple immigrated to Northern Rhodesia (Zambia) where their three sons were born. When their youngest son developed primary bone cancer, Sheila sat at his hospital bedside and was impelled by the drama of this situation to write about the incredible battle they fought together. This true and thought-provoking story, *Fly With a Miracle*, was later re-published under the title *Count to Ten*, by Taylor Street Books in San Francisco, where until April 2014 Sheila was chief editor. Second editions of her four novels to date have now been published by Precious Oil Publications. Sheila and Colin spend six months of the year in Cape Town, the other six in Menorca and the UK. She loves music, photography, walking and dancing. Her love for ballet never left her and this love has inspired a number of her books.

Also by Sheila Mary Taylor:

Pinpoint

Count to Ten

Dance to a Tangled Web

Golden Sapphire

Lari's Castle

Books edited by Sheila Belshaw

Kathie

Don't Tread on My Dreams

Rage of Life

(by Dora Taylor and published posthumously

by Penguin)

ELDORADO

A Fable

Sheila Mary Taylor

Bardel Publishing

A Bardel Publication

Published by Bardel 2015
© Sheila Mary Taylor 2012 and 2015

First published in 2012 by Taylor Street Publishing, San Francisco
Second revised edition published in 2015 by Bardel Publishing

No part of this book may be reproduced or transmitted in any form or by any means, electronic or mechanical, including photocopying, recording, or by any information storage and retrieval system, without permission in writing from the publisher
This is a work of fiction. Names, places, businesses, characters and incidents are either the product of the author's imagination or are used fictitiously, and any resemblance to any actual persons, living or dead, organisations, events or locales, or any other entity, is entirely coincidental. The unauthorised reproduction or distribution of this copyrighted work is illegal.

Cover designed by Bardel
Image © Sheila Mary Taylor

This story is in loving memory of my mother, Dora Taylor, whose childhood of abuse and cruelty inspired her goal in life to do everything in her power to help others less fortunate than herself, and who succumbed at far too early an age to an illness that could have been cured.

Oft have I pondered in the night's silence,
Dry-eyed,
Wide-eyed in the whirling dark,
Of all that man suffers between waking and sleep,
Between the hour of innocent birth
And stark death,
Vanishing, empty-handed,
Strengthless as a shadow,
Alone in his going, as he came,
Alone.

From 'Tristan & Iseult' by Dora Taylor

Gold.

Gold is why everyone is here in Tarkwa: my long suffering, pain-ridden mother; my hard-working engineer father, still a stranger to me; the Johnsons, the Smiths, the Elliots and the Harmans who drink themselves silly at the Club every night; Joseph our cook, who produces culinary surprises worthy of the Ritz, and David our driver – our lifeline to the world outside of this magical house on stilts that commands a view not only over all of Tarkwa but of the myriad surrounding villages and the hills of gold; John, our gentle steward, who washes and irons in the red mud-laden Tarkwa water all our clothes, bedding and towels, which emerge each day as though newly bought, even though the whites will never be white again. And the thousands of other Ghanaians who toil in the mines, who run the banks and the Government offices, who tend the myriad shanty shops and the ramshackle markets.

Even the galampsays.

Gold is what keeps us all alive – some more than others.

* * *

From the veranda of our house perched high on the crest of the hill to catch the breezes and escape the worst of the mosquitoes, I gaze across the verdant hills to the hazy horizon.

A huge yellow sun blazes in a shimmering sky. Bamboo leaves shiver and palm fronds clatter and bees buzz busily around brilliant red hibiscus and pink frangipanis. Drums beat and hooters hoot. Cocks crow and crows squawk. Crickets screech and melodious bulbuls tell each other, 'I'm a pretty bird.' And all around me the sound of people drifts up from lush green valleys. Happy people. People laughing and talking. People playing music. People singing and dancing.

Ghana.

The Gold Coast, they used to call it. Not only because of the richness of its mineral wealth but for the outrageous selling of thousands of their own people to work as slaves on distant shores.

But listen. One sound drowns all others. The over-riding clanking and clashing that has been going on twenty-four hours a day for as long as I can remember: the sound of rocks and stones being struck and pounded by hammers and metal pipes – the sound of the galampsays, the 'illegal' miners extracting gold from the rocks they bring up at dead of night from secret tunnels they think nobody knows about; the illegal miners who risk their lives scrounging for the precious metal on the fringes of all the gold mines of Ghana – and all over mineral-rich

Africa. Illegal now, because the mining rights have all been bought by rich international mining companies, but hardly illegal when you know that the Ghanaians have been toiling for gold from their rivers and hills in one way or another for thousands of years.

I breathe in the gorgeous fresh smell of Ghana. Oh, if only I could stay here forever – the land of my birth. The only land I feel I belong to. But today, if the ever watchful authorities get wind of what I am planning to do, my right to live here in this paradise might be threatened.

The Ghanaians are a proud people. If word got out that I was trying to do something that at first they might misunderstand, that they might misconstrue as being taking undue advantage of my privilege of citizenship; that they might feel had no ultimate merit for the well-being of Ghanaians, it might be – it could be – the last time I would be able to soak up the sights and smells and sounds that would shape my memories when I am far, far away ...

* * *

It's too soon to tell whether the giant pharmaceutical company will respond to the unorthodox plan Adam and I are about to set in motion – illegal some might say. Or whether the project will fail miserably. But if word of my involvement gets out and is misinterpreted, I'd be deported and might never be able to come back. I've heard of people bundled on to the first available plane amid hushed accusing whispers, for far lesser crimes, never to be seen again in Tarkwa town, or anywhere else in Ghana.

But I am not afraid. I am driven by a compulsion far stronger than fear. And who would suspect an intelligent, softly spoken girl, so kind and thoughtful for her twenty-two years? Well, isn't that what everyone says about me? Even to my face, though what they say behind my back may be quite different. This small group of expatriates who work far from home have little else to talk about – except all the other expatriates. It is a life far from reality, a life where most of them live in 'cloud-cuckoo-land'. A life so different from their own humdrum lives in England or Canada or Australia that allows them to engage sometimes in escapades they would not dream of doing anywhere else.

I smile to myself. There you are, Nikki. You are your own alibi. And, as Adam said to me, "If all goes well, Nikki, ah, think what a revolutionary change it would make to the thousands of people suffering the way your mother is suffering. And think what a sense of fulfilment you will have."

Fulfilment! I had looked at Adam, frowning, wondering, trying to work out what this '*sense of fulfilment*' really meant.

* * *

A car hoots at the back door. I take a slow deep breath hoping it will give me courage, aware that I'm about to embark upon the most significant episode of my life.

"If you're going into town, Nikki dear ..."

It's what my mother always says whenever she hears the sound of Dad's car coming up the hill, knowing it isn't Dad as he never comes home during a working day, but knowing it is David coming to take me shopping or visiting a friend. I could almost recite the words with which Mum would complete her request, because these days it's as if she has run out of words, so the few she utters never differ.

"... please buy some carrots, some really fresh juicy ones, darling, that have just been dug up this morning. Your father's stomach is upset again and carrots are the only thing he can tolerate. Carrots and rice. No wonder he's losing so much weight."

My mother's thin voice comes plaintively

from the reclining chair to which she is confined these days, except when we help her to bed at night. "I don't feel like going out in this heat just for carrots," she adds light-heartedly. But light-hearted is the last thing that Mum feels. Mum is making a huge effort to sound as normal as possible. There is no way she is able to go out anywhere, even if she wanted to. Her condition has worsened so much, even in the few days I've been back in Ghana, that I am torn between staying at home to be with her and look after her – and doing what just might save her life and thousands of others like her.

If the galampsays cooperate.

I pick up my blue canvas shoulder bag, large enough to take the enormous wads of devalued *cedis* we must all carry around these days, and large enough for the precious cargo I'll be collecting from Adam, though I have no idea how large this will be. Before going to the front door, I go to my mother. As I hold her hand, giving it a gentle squeeze to tell her I love her, I look at her shiny putty-coloured face and a pang of pity overcomes me.

"Mum", I say. "Why don't you and Dad go back to England where there's a good hospital —"

I bite my tongue when I realise what I've said. How could I forget it had been Mum's dream to own a little house in Brighton with a sea view and a little garden where she could grow roses and pansies? How thoughtless to come out with it now, when I'm sure Dad has no intention of buying a house in Brighton, or anywhere else in England or the rest of the world. 'What's wrong with Ghana?' he always used to say, genuinely surprised that Gillian didn't share his love of heat and humidity and rain and thunder and sudden loss of electricity, and his apparent indifference to mould and dirt and rats and ants and cockroaches. The list of things Mum hates about Ghana is endless, but lately she doesn't complain about them much. It's as though she has resigned herself to her fate. It's as though she knows it is too late to change anything. Or is this merely a natural tool the brain uses to ensure acceptance of the body's inevitable slowing down process when nothing can be done to save it?

"That's a crazy idea, Nikki," Mum says, mopping her brow with one of the pile of white cotton handkerchiefs on the little mahogany table next to her chair – fine white cotton handkerchiefs that Joseph launders every day because Mum thinks tissues are a waste of money.

"What do you think would happen to Kwame Mine, Nikki? Everyone says your father's the best engineer they've ever had." This is Gillian's favourite subject, and she loses no opportunity to expound it.

"Bradley … Parker …" She says his name slowly, with such pride, looking up at the ceiling, a faint smile creasing her pale face, "… has trebled production, stream-lined the operation and eradicated almost all the gold theft." She sighs with the immense satisfaction it gives her that Dad is so highly respected in this small mining community.

And I know in a further flash of pity that this pride in her husband is what must have made her put up with Ghana all these years, pushing the dream of her little house in Brighton firmly into the realm of her fantasies.

She takes a long deep breath. "Such an honest, hardworking man would be impossible to replace."

I bend to kiss her, closing my eyes as I think how lucky I am to be able to do this. For so many days of every year I am thousands of miles away from her and I don't think she realises how much I miss her or how much I have always missed her ever since I was sent to boarding school at the age of eight.

She smiles and I kiss her again, holding back my tears. She never tells me she loves me but at moments like this I have a warm feeling inside me that perhaps she does.

As I hover in the doorway, reluctant to leave her but eager to keep my exciting rendezvous with Adam, she shakes her head. "Impossible – to – replace," she repeats slowly.

Mum does everything slowly now. She says that in the hot weather it conserves energy, although for me the more active I am the less time I have to think about the heat.

But it's different for poor Mum. And it's still hard for me to accept that she is so ill. Dad refuses to talk about it. But you don't need a doctor to tell you she is going downhill fast. When Dad phoned me at uni saying I should come home for Christmas – as if I would dream of going anywhere else – because he was worried about Gillian's deterioration in health, my anger rose. "Can't the doctors do something?" I asked him. "They've done everything they can," he said. "There's nothing more to do." Oh, God! I had thought helplessly. Why isn't there a cure? It's so unfair. *If only there were something I could do ...*

There must be something I can do.

"David's waiting for me, Mum. See you later." I must never let her know how worried I am. She wouldn't like that and it would undermine any confidence she might still harbour that she would recover. Because that's Mum. And at times I'm sure I can detect in her expression a look that tells me she has no intention of dying.

"Don't go talking to anybody you don't know, Nikki, dear."

I blow her a kiss, not wanting to upset her but silently acknowledging the same words she has uttered every time I've left this house since I was old enough to go out on my own. She just doesn't understand how different the Ghanaians are from English people. They are so friendly that it's impossible not to speak to them. And in Ghana it's considered impolite not to greet someone who greets you, whether you know them or not. Just yesterday, as I strolled through the shady footpaths leading down into

Tarkwa town, I came face to face with a group of laughing children on their way to school. 'Hello, *bruni,* how are you? I am fine," they said in unison, *bruni* being the local word for an expatriate, a white person. How could you not respond to such friendliness without a smile and a similar greeting?

Besides, who else can I talk to? I've nothing whatsoever in common with the Johnsons, the Smiths, the Elliots or the Harmans. They are good people doing an amazing job just as Dad does, but we are worlds' apart.

David opens the car door. "Good morning, Nikki, how are you?" he says, with a wide grin and a slight tilt of his head that I am never sure means he expects me to say I am fine, or that I am fed up with all the negatives most expatriates cannot help expounding upon, but which for me, whether he knows it or not, are non-existent.

I return the greeting and settle myself in the seat next to him. "Take me to Kotonka, please

David," I say firmly, trying to hide the quiver of excitement in my voice as the car weaves waveringly down the narrow, twisting, pot-holed road into the sprawling, bustling, colourful town called Tarkwa.

David flicks his eyes at me then flicks them back to the road, as if to say: *Kotonka? Not to the market for oranges and tomatoes and pineapples? Or Quality Stores for printed cottons? Or The Lord is My Shepherd for rice and sugar? What has got into Nikki today? It's a dreadful journey through dense forest and will take two and a half hours. And when you get there, what is there to do?*

But all he says is: "Yes, Nikki," wiping the sweat from the back of his neck and jabbing the air-conditioning button on full to emphasise how tedious such a journey is going to be, and probably wishing I'd said Prestea Mine, high up in the hills, where there's a sparkling pool. Or even Kwame Mine where Dad works, only ten miles on a good dirt road. But he shrugs amiably, and the gesture reminds me of the time he told me he would do anything for me because I was different from the others. "You're almost like a Ghanaian, Nikki," he had said. "The way you always think of other people, doing things for them and giving them things you can't afford, like the books you bought for my children."

    I had been embarrassed at this frank outburst, his one and only in all the years I've known him, but somehow it brought us much closer. Like real friends – not just for the moment but for always. I too would do anything for David.

What a journey this is! I'm so excited I'm almost oblivious of the impenetrable jungle towering above the car on either side of the road, displaying every possible shade of green from the palest delicate to the boldest bold in the spectrum. The clumps of spiky bamboo, the fan palms and the coconut palms and the elegant royal palms with their artificial plastic leaves and their trunks so neat, and the tall cotton trees – all meshed together by a thick weave of all-encompassing clinging creepers.

   I don't care how much the car bounces and rocks over the rough road. In a few hours Adam will be handing over the gold, and I'll be putting it into my blue canvas bag. I've never wanted anything so much in all my life. Not for myself, of course, although I do love gold. Gold can flatter you, but you have to look right before it can do that. Like no amount of gold jewellery can do anything for my mother now. But if I've been to Busua Beach for the day, and come back with a tan and my hair bleached by the sun, and if there's a party that night and I wear my gold chain and my gold earrings inherited from my mother's mother, I know I look good because the gold is clever the way it sets off the gleam of my blonde hair and the glow of my cheeks and even the blue of my eyes. Yes, I do like gold, and for a moment I allow myself a rare fantasy. Wouldn't it be nice just once to go to Marks and Spencer's before my flight to Ghana at the end of term, to splash out on a smart new dress that my gold chain would enhance – instead of having to buy a cheap length of Ghana printed cotton from Quality Stores, which a seamstress treadling her ancient Singer by the side of a dusty road would make up for me, with the same round neck and tent shape Mum and I always wear that keeps you cool but hides the shape of your breasts? Only there are no breasts now for my mother's shapeless dress to hide.

I can never understand why lately the Parker family always seems hard-up compared to other families. In the past it was never like this. Dad gets paid well, so where does all the money go? Why doesn't he give Mum more money for our daily needs? "Don't waste any of that yeast, Joseph," my mother says, when it costs hardly anything and she should be thankful that Joseph bakes such delicious bread in our big steaming kitchen so that we don't have to eat the strangely sweet Ghanaian bread.

But that's just wishful thinking. The gold I will get today is different.

* * *

My mind darts back to the Ghana Airways flight just over a week ago, when I was propositioned. The tall slender young man sitting next to me in the window seat said in perfect English and with a friendly smile as all Ghanaians do, "Hello, how are you?" and then we talked non-stop for the whole six hours from Heathrow to Accra. Six hours doesn't seem very long to have made such momentous plans with a perfect stranger.

He asked me far more questions than I asked him, but in such a friendly way that it never made me feel uncomfortable. His name is Adam Afari, a research chemist: young, enthusiastic and forward thinking, working for a giant pharmaceutical company in Europe. Just before landing at Accra he held out his hand with yet another dazzling smile which showed a row of Colgate-perfect teeth set against the smooth ebony of his skin, and I responded with the traditional West African handshake ending with the terminal finger snap, sealing our friendship and our new partnership.

Walking down the aircraft steps to be enveloped in a blanket of hot humid air, so delicious after the biting cold of England's winter, I glanced back to nod at Adam having agreed that we should not be seen together in the airport building, and it struck me that he had postulated the most wonderful idea I had ever heard.

It was the miracle I'd been hoping for. Something I could do to help – not only my mother but thousands of other cancer sufferers with no cure in sight.

Nobody in their right senses would turn it down. The successful outcome could do nothing but good, I told myself as I walked down the long, reeking corridor where the Immigration and Health Officers check your passport and make sure you're inoculated against yellow fever, cholera and typhoid. I've never been ill with any tropical disease, not even malaria. Nor have Mum and Dad, probably because we eat copious amounts of pineapples which grow everywhere, even in our garden like rows of miniature palm trees, and are now rumoured to have astounding properties with the power to prevent malaria.

* * *

"Nearly there, Nikki," David says as we approach the outskirts of Kotonka.

And I am shocked by the moon-like vista facing

me – the devastation of the surrounding forest caused by the gigantic open pit mine – the ravages of which are as evil as the annihilation of the priceless rain forests by the loggers felling beautiful trees for export to countries who have no feeling for the consequences. I remember Adam telling me with tears in his eyes how this was affecting much of life in Ghana. "At first I didn't believe what the researchers were telling us," he said. "But they have found that cutting down the beautiful tall trees in our rainforests can actually affect the rainfall not only in the forests but in the surrounding areas. Many Ghanaians would starve as they rely on rain for their livelihoods." Adam had closed his eyes and screwed up his face. "Surely everyone knows that trees give moisture to the air through their leaves …"

I hold on tightly as David slows down to negotiate an enormous pot-hole – a crater which spans the whole width of the road, remembering Adam telling me that not so very long ago rain forests covered about twenty percent of the earth and now they cover only five percent. "Greed," he had said, wiping a tear from his cheek. "And if only they realised that every time they cut down a tree the special soil gets washed away when it rains, so that new trees are unable to grow there."

"I'm meeting a friend at the Club," I tell David as though it's the most normal thing to do on a Tuesday morning in a mining town I never visit.

David must wonder why I didn't tell him who I was going to meet. He knows all our friends, and none of them live or work in Kotonka. But he says nothing. He drives us everywhere. He drives Dad every day to Kwame Mine and back again, although he is often dismissed early when Dad tells him he is working late and doesn't want to keep him hanging around and gives him a handful of *cedis* to get a ride back to Tarkwa on a mammy-wagon – one of those ancient old-fashioned wooden trucks with the obligatory sign-boards every tro-tro displays:

'*God is Good*'. '*Jesus is Life*'. '*Life is war*'. '*No money, no friend ...*'

David also used to drive my mother on shopping trips to Takoradi or Accra, and sometimes at weekends to Busua Beach. He assumes it isn't for him to question the reason for these trips, although I'm sure he always knows.

Except on this momentous day.

The moment I enter the building I spot Adam. He is in the far corner of the bleak dusty room, talking animatedly to a group of men clustered round a beer-stained wooden table. There's a sudden silence as all eyes turn towards me.

Wearing a fresh white shirt and tight jeans, he hurries over with outstretched arms. "Come, we can talk over here." He grasps my hand and leads me to a table on the opposite side of the room from the group of men.

Directly above us a noisy ceiling fan whirls and clatters. A smell of stale beer and cigarette smoke hits my nostrils.

Adam pulls out a battered wooden chair for me and places his chair with the back facing me. He straddles the chair, leans his arms on the back and smiles, though for some reason the smile does not seem as deep as the smiles he had for me on the six-hour flight from Heathrow.

I hold my breath, waiting for him to speak. I gaze at the smoothness of his skin, stretched over the high cheek bones. The sweat begins to trickle down my back.

"I wasn't sure you'd come," he says at last. "I'm glad you could make it."

"Adam," I say under my breath, "surely we can't talk here …"

"Why not? This is a Mine Club. The non-stop racket will drown our voices. Don't worry, Nikki. Anywhere else would be suspect."

The smile suddenly leaves his face and he says, "I'm afraid it's hopeless." He frowns and slowly shakes his head from side to side.

"These people used to be so ... what do you say ... accommodating. I don't know what's wrong with them now."

I purse my lips to hide the surge of disappointment that sweeps through my body. This news is so unexpected that I don't know what to say. He lowers his voice. "Maybe I've been away too long and they don't trust me anymore. I've talked to them for two days but they're like a mountain. You can't move them. And I know they have it. Plenty of it. They just won't lend it to us even though I've promised them a far better return than they would get from the Lebanese crooks who pay them a pittance for their gold. Perhaps the authorities are watching and they're afraid."

A sinking feeling of failure floods my chest. "It doesn't matter, Adam. Maybe we were too ambitious. And anyway, it's illegal."

"Shh!" Adam makes a hissing sound as he glances over his shoulder towards the group of men who thankfully all seem to be talking at once. "That's one word you must not say." He lets out a long sigh, then wipes the beads of perspiration from his forehead. "Look, all we're doing is forcing – no, not forcing, we are trying to convince this enormously wealthy company I work for to do something it should already have done as a matter of principle, no matter what the cost. Instead of pandering to their greedy shareholders they should think only of the patients needing their drugs. Anyway, once we've given them the opportunity to make the tests and they can see for themselves what a miracle is in front of their noses, I'm sure they'll be prepared to pay the right kind of money for such a prize. They'll be criminal if they don't. Then we'll be able to pay back these people what we owe them."

"Have you explained all this to the galampsays?"

"I've told them that if they'll just let us have the gold now, as a loan, they'll eventually be far richer than if they went on mining until they die, selling their gold to the traders who exploit them so outrageously. Except they might have to wait a little while for their money."

"And are you sure the Kondahene will only accept gold as payment?" I ask him, feeling sick with the thought of our plans being thwarted.

"Nothing else will be considered." Adam's face is contorted with the pain of frustration. "Paper money loses its value too quickly these days. And the Kondahene needs money to keep the plunderers of the forest at bay. This is his most important goal as leader of our people. The whole future of Ghana could be at stake if the greedy felling of trees continues."

I wait for him to continue, as I know how deeply he feels about this threat. But he presses his lips together, closes his eyes and looks down at his feet.

"Oh, well, then that's that, I suppose." I stand up and peel my soggy cotton skirt away from the backs of my legs, suddenly wanting to get back to my mother as quickly as possible, wanting desperately to do something – anything to help her now that this plan has failed so miserably. And remembering that there are still the carrots to buy.

Adam looks up at me. I gaze into his eyes, drawn together now in a deep frown of disappointment. "Perhaps we'll meet again," I say, trying to smile, trying to stop the trembling of my bottom lip when I think of my mother, doomed now to her inevitable fate. It was always a long chance, I tell myself, especially when I realise just how far downhill she has gone since last August when she saw me off at the airport. But anything would be better than watching while she fades before my eyes. And there is always the thought of the thousands of others we could be helping. I shake my head as I feel my eyes mist over.

I'm about to walk away when Adam clutches my arm.

"Wait! Maybe ... maybe there is another

way."

I hold my breath. It looks as though he is not prepared to give up so soon after all, but as I watch his face light up again, I think perhaps it's only his innate Ghanaian optimism giving him fresh impetus to clutch at straws.

"There is just one more faint chance," he says, enunciating the words slowly and deliberately as though to make them more credible.

I blink my eyes as I wait.

"It was something one of these men said about somebody they knew of … somebody who they thought might be able to help." He gestures towards the corner. "Give me a couple of days, Nikki. It's worth trying. Can I phone you at home?" His dark brown eyes are hopeful once more.

I had stipulated from the start I didn't want Adam to contact me. He doesn't know my surname and that's the way it has to continue. I can't risk being traced to this transaction.

Anything that looked vaguely illicit on my part would be extremely detrimental to my father's position of trust at Kwame Mine. I cannot risk jeopardising his career, his livelihood, his reputation. I know how much he loves his job, though I can never understand why a senior engineer should work such long overtime hours – far more than other mine employees do, coming home late at night while his colleagues play golf or darts or snooker and drink beer till silly-o-clock at the Club. No. It's absolutely essential that nobody should know about my involvement. It's a big country but news travels fast. If you aren't careful everybody knows everything about you – sometimes even before you do.

"No, Adam. You'll have to tell me now where and when to meet you. And don't forget I'm flying back on the fifth of January. There's not much time. I can't leave any later and if I still have to travel north to do the deal with the Kondahene …"

Adam takes both my hands in his. "Trust me, Nikki. I want this as much as you do. Remember that. And we're partners." He draws me closer. "You're not getting cold feet, are you?" he asks, his mouth drooping at the corners, so different from his usual wide, sunny smile.

"No, of course not. But I thought today and the day I travel to the Kondahene with the gold would be the only two days I'd have to make excuses to my Dad about where I've been. It's not easy to do it often. And I don't like leaving my mother."

A successful mission today would have given me the self-assurance to make up a plausible excuse for my forthcoming long journey to the Kondahene. I'm not sure I can do it a second time.

Adam narrows his eyes. "Do you know the Jesus Lives Beauty Salon, behind the market in Tarkwa?"

"Umm ... Yes, I think I know it." Somehow I

single the place out in my mind's eye from the hundreds of small shanty establishments in the dusty maze of Tarkwa town, by its short white net curtain drawn across the entrance and its electric pink sign, just past The Lord is My Shepherd.

"In two days' time," he says. "Go there for a manicure. Rosie will give you a piece of paper."

"Rosie? Okay. And if we get the gold, when will I hand it over to the Kondahene?" The adrenaline has begun to flow again. It's all I can do to keep from throwing my arms around Adam's neck.

"I will arrange it, Nikki. Don't worry. Just be at the Jesus Lives Beauty Salon by twelve noon in two days' time."

"I'll be there," I say, my heart singing.

With my pulse racing and my stomach churning with excitement, I turn and walk across the room. I know that all eyes are riveted on my back. I'm tempted to turn and wave to Adam – even to blow him a kiss as I'm so happy. They probably already think we're lovers, I muse, curbing my temptation. Oh God, what if it gets to Mum's ears? Or Dad's? They're so old-fashioned they still think I'm too young for that sort of thing.

But that would be better than anybody knowing what we're really doing. Or rather, what we're being forced to do in order to achieve our goal and kick-start the money-grabbing pharmaceutical company. Until this goal is successfully realised, nobody will understand.

* * *

David holds open the car door. A wave of heat hits me as I slide onto the front seat and I'm thankful when we get away and the air-conditioner blows an ice-cold draught onto my face and up the sides of my legs.

"Where to now, Nikki?" he asks.

"Tarkwa market for carrots, and then home,

please, David." I avoid his glances and try to slow down my breathing. Adam had remained inside the Club, so David can be none the wiser about my clandestine meeting with the young chemist.

Miraculously the return journey takes only two and a quarter hours, in spite of the stop to buy carrots and as an afterthought a few tomatoes which the amiable seller wraps neatly in a large banana leaf, adding an extra tomato at the last minute, smiling at me as she says, "Dash for you." It works both ways in Ghana. You do me a good turn and this will ensure that I will do you a favour in return.

Even so, it is with trepidation that I step out of the car to greet my mother, urging David to hurry to Kwame Mine on the off-chance that Dad might need his car early.

Mum doesn't seem to have moved in the six hours I've been away from the house, except that she looks even more uncomfortable than she did before, though I'm certain Joseph will have been watching her carefully. Joseph is the kindest, most thoughtful person on this earth. He lives in a large room underneath our house. Not long ago he rescued a litter of kittens after a fight in which the mother cat was killed. He took them into his room, made a nest for them in an old basket, bought milk for them and frequently invited me down to his room to show me how they were thriving. It was a lovely sight to see the way he stroked them and cuddled them.

"Where on earth have you been, Nikki dear?" Mum asks. "I've been worried out of my mind."

But I'm already in the bathroom running the cold tap, wetting one of the flannels which always hang over the edge of the bath. I squeeze it out and place it on Mum's brow. "You know what the roads are like, Mum. I went to Prestea to see the Jacksons. But they had travelled to Accra." I'm surprised at how easily the lie slides off my lips. "It seemed a pity to waste the journey, so I carried on to Kotonka to see Frank Jones. He sat behind me in the plane from London and was moaning about having nobody his age to talk to since moving to Kotonka. Well, it was nice to see him."

Another lie, and just as easy as the first. Luckily I'd noticed boring Frank sitting a few rows behind me in the plane. Not the kind of person I would ever spend two hours bumping and bouncing around in a car for. But it seems to satisfy Mum. I gaze at the tired face, more relaxed now with the evaporation of the wet cloth cooling her head.

"Have you had a pain pill, Mum?"

She runs her fingers through her thin, damp, straggly hair, such a contrast to the thick lustrous reddish-brown hair she used to have. Gillian never discusses her illness or the pain because she believes you have to keep this kind of thing to yourself.

"I don't need one, Nikki," she answers, twisting her emaciated body in an attempt to ease her discomfort. "Joseph offered them to me several times when he brought my tea, but I declined them."

Why, I wonder? Why does she deny herself the relief?

"What about supper? Are we waiting for Dad tonight?"

She brushes imaginary gecko droppings from the mahogany coffee table at her side. "I've told Joseph we'll eat at six-thirty as usual, after the news. Your father will have his carrots and rice whenever he comes in," she adds.

She looks up at me. "You didn't tell me you were so friendly with the Jones boy. What's he like?"

"He's all right, Mum. He's reading Economics at Southampton University." That's all I know about Frank Jones and my mother doesn't need to know any more. It's better to say nothing than to say the wrong thing.

"Well, that's nice …" She is too tired for conversation. I don't even need to fabricate a huge lie. Two little ones have done the trick.

* * *

I go to my chair over-looking the green hills and the sprawling town of Tarkwa, thinking about the day's disappointing outcome. I watch two crows squabble over the last morsel of potato peelings Joseph has thrown over the edge of the slope. Gillian was at first horrified by this seemingly unhygienic, un-British habit, but had soon learned that in Ghana nothing is ever wasted; even empty bottles and plastic bags are fought over and sold in town for profit. I peep through the louvers and see that Mum is sleeping peacefully, so I stay to watch the sun plunge behind the layer of dry desert dust the Harmattan blows from the Sahara in the dry season. I go round the house closing the curtains to keep out the quickly darkening sky – quicker than anywhere else I know as we are almost slap bang right on the equator. Gillian hates a dark sky. A relic from her childhood in England, I expect, where winter closes in at four in the afternoon. But I love to see the sky explode from blue to grey, to orange to dark blue to purple, the way it does nowhere else so spectacularly as in tropical Africa.

When Joseph rings the little silver bell I help Mum to the table. It's difficult for her to sit in an upright chair but she is always determined to try.

"Is there anything else you'd like?" I ask when she puts down her knife and fork, her plate hardly touched.

"Just some pawpaw, dear. Joseph knows."

I'm thankful that she likes pawpaw. I've read somewhere that doctors think it is one of the wonder foods of this tropical paradise. The leafy trees grow in the garden and we eat almost as much of the delicious orange flesh of the pawpaw as we do the tangy pineapples. But after two bites of her pawpaw Gillian slides awkwardly to the edge of her chair, holding on to the polished wooden arm-rests.

"I think I'll go to bed now," she says, closing her eyes. "These chairs are so uncomfortable …"

It would be unkind to remind her of how thrilled she had been when she bought the chairs five years ago on the outskirts of Accra, making David screech to a halt when she saw them displayed in the mud alongside the main coastal highway. "The Ghanaians know how to make chairs, I must give them their due," she had said. "And I just love mahogany."

I had not shared her enthusiasm. "They're destroying the rain forests by cutting down all those trees," I had told her, having just done the Rain Forests in my Geography class.

"Oh, they'll grow again," she said. "Remember those poles we erected for a washing line? Within weeks they sprouted leaves! Everything grows faster here than you can see it."

"But never quite the same again," I had

insisted, having seen countless enormous lorries thundering through the town on the way to the coast, laden with the tall, noble trees of the forests. "And some precious plants in the forests are lost forever. They're unable to re-seed because they don't have sufficient canopy left to protect them."

I assist the ever faithful Joseph to help her to bed. I struggle to hold back sudden tears as I see the frail body revealed beneath the shapeless dress, nothing left but skin and bone. I tuck her in. She asks me to close the window.

"The galampsays make so much noise, clanking down there in the valley," she says. "Day in, day out. I don't know why they carry on mining when they know it's illegal. Do you know that one of them accidentally popped out of a hole in the Smith's garden the other day. A tunnel that had gone way off line!"

She laughs and I laugh with her. She so

seldom laughs.

"I've always rather liked the sound the galampsays make, Mum –" I stop myself just in time from telling her I like the sound even more now because it's part of our wonderful plan. Without the galampsays …

"I don't know how they get away with it," Gillian goes on, closing her eyes.

* * *

The night has a stillness I've never noticed before. A stillness like the moment before a storm that seems to herald what is soon to burst forth. The house is silent except for the whirring of ceiling fans and the hum of air-conditioners. Outside in the lush greenery a thousand crickets screech. The haunting sound of nightlife music drifts up from Cyanide, the village from which on a Sunday I love to hear the harmony of a dozen different church choirs wafting up the valley.

With my legs curled under me on the mahogany chair, welcoming the opportunity to wait up for my father, I settle down with the latest Wilbur Smith novel somebody on the plane had given me. I've hardly seen Dad since arriving home and tonight I feel the need to talk to him. The pain-killer Mum has to take at night ensures she has a good sleep.

I'm almost asleep myself when I hear the car coming up the hill. Joseph, who waits patiently for Brad's arrival every night, puts the carrots and rice and a fresh jug of iced water on the dining-room table.

I look at my watch and wonder what it is that drives my father. Surely no job should keep a man out of his home for more than twelve hours a day.

"Hello, Dad," I say as he walks in and puts down the black leather briefcase he always carries with him, never letting it out of his sight.

He seems startled, lost in his own world.

"Oh, you're still up."

I can't think why he should be surprised. He knows I hate going to bed early. But neither he nor Mum has the slightest idea about today's younger generation. It's almost as though they've never been young themselves. I try imagining what he'd have been like at my age. He is so undemonstrative, even with Mum, yet he must have loved her then, and in his own way I guess he still does, if worrying about someone can be called loving. Yet never once have I heard either of them tell each other that they do. I've never heard them express any personal sentiment whatsoever.

"I can't go to bed early, Dad. My air-conditioner's broken and the fan isn't much good either." I don't tell him I want to talk to him because that might make him close up even more. "Did you have a good day at work?" I say as he sits down in front of his steaming carrots and rice.

The question surprises him and he looks up.

"The same," he says, shrugging his shoulders and staring once more into the mound of rice. Then he looks at me. "How was Mum today?"

He must know from David's mileage report that I've been to Kotonka and that it must have taken me away from the house for most of the day, yet he chooses not to comment on that. Not that he ever does comment on things, so I suspect, rightly or wrongly, that there is some reason why he is trying to catch me out.

"I think she had quite a lot of pain," I venture. "She didn't eat much of her dinner." I often wish he would show some consternation on his face, anything rather than the blank expression that seldom changes. He has one of those perfectly balanced faces that never looks tired or bloated or sad, and certainly never dissipated. I size up the widely spaced dark blue eyes, the straight blond hair, still thick and shiny, with no sign of baldness or grey. He must have been a real killer when he was my age. His firm jaw line gives him a toughness that matches his enduring tenacity, but somehow it doesn't gel with his apparent lack of determination to make something more of his personal position in life.

As though he can read my thoughts, he suddenly looks up and stares directly into my eyes.

"What is it, Nikki? What are you up to?"

His words take my breath away. For a moment I wonder why I don't just come out with it, but an embarrassing flush spreads unheralded from my neck, up and over my cheeks and forehead and for once I'm thankful for Tarkwa's perennially dim light bulbs. It takes me by surprise that my father is more perceptive than I had imagined. To get over the awkward moment I reach for the glass of fresh orange juice Joseph has squeezed for me. How I wish I could tell him. Make him part of the plan. If he was any other kind of father I would be able to confide in him but I know that would be impossible. He would never condone such a scheme.

"Nothing, Dad. Why do you ask?" He surely can't know anything. Nobody knows except Adam, and he is just as keen to keep my involvement a secret – at this stage anyway, although I'm still going to be the one who has to finalise the deal with the Kondahene. Adam insisted that he should not be involved in that delicate step of the proceedings, although he has done all the groundwork and made arrangements for the eventual specialised shipment of the precious plant. He had explained to me that he was on a special mission for his company which directly involved the Ghanaian Government, and that when he had tentatively raised the subject during his briefing in London with the Trade people at the High Commission, they had told him to forget it. "You see," he'd explained to me, "there are some traditional things in Ghana which have persisted in spite of the long contact with European cultural forms, but these are for Ghanaians only: well guarded, not to be shared or traded. But we, as research chemists, would be failing in our duty to mankind if we didn't try to capture and synthesise these unique plants from one of the only surviving areas of virgin rain forest which has been so carefully guarded by the Kondahene."

His vision had captured my imagination.

"I know you, my girl," Dad says softly. "And there's been a strange, far-away look in your eyes ever since I picked you up at the airport."

I pretend not to understand him. I don't think there's any point in trying to explain.

Joseph tip-toes in and removes the half-eaten plate of carrots and rice and replaces it with a colourful dish of pineapples, oranges, pawpaws and bananas. Dad looks up at him as if to say, 'Not again'. But he says nothing and picks up his spoon.

"People in England would pay a fortune for an exotic fruit salad like that," I can't help saying. "Our fruit is juicier, sweeter, more flavourful than any other I've tasted. And we eat it every day for next to nothing. I wonder what it is about Ghana that makes the fruit taste so fantastic."

Dad smiles, no doubt recognising that I am merely repeating a question Gillian so often asks him. And yet it almost feels as though we've reached a point of contact.

"The soil is rich from all the rotting vegetation," he says, "and the rain and sun come in exactly the right proportions. It couldn't be simpler." He has a sudden far-away look. "I always think of the hymn we sang when I was at school. *We plough the fields and scatter ...*"

But, as if he is embarrassed at disclosing this memory, his voice trails into silence, though his words have triggered an avalanche of questions in my head.

Will Adam's huge pharmaceutical company be able to reproduce the same perfect environment for the laboratory growth of the magical plant we're hoping to inveigle the Kondahene into selling to us? It would be a tragedy if they can't. And what if the plant refuses to be genetically coded, or whatever it is that scientists do to mimic its growth? And what if they aren't able to transfer it to a micro-organism so that it can be mass produced? What if the rain forest is the only place it can thrive? And what if Adam and I pay out all that gold that we could never afford to buy ourselves – hence the desperate need to borrow it – and it all comes to nothing?

Hell, why doesn't the bloody pharmaceutical company have the guts to buy the goddam plant themselves, no matter what the cost? Aren't they rich enough already? Their selfish wealth and the greed of their shareholders disgust me. All they think about is profit – not helping the people who are in dire need of their revoltingly expensive medications. For them it's just a commercial product they're manufacturing, not a life-saving miracle. Their goals are all wrong.

I keep as normal an expression as possible

while the thoughts of possible failure race through my mind. It seems strange that I cannot confide in my father. Not that I intend breathing a word to him about what is going on but at least I had hoped to find out something about the Konda people and in particular their tribal chief, the Kondahene. Dad has worked for years in Ghana and knows a lot about the people. But now that he has hinted to me that he has wind of something unusual in the air, there is no way I can ask a single question without arousing his suspicions even more.

Quickly I change the subject. "Is Mum going to get better, Dad?"

I know that without a miracle, she is not going to get better, but I desperately want to know from Dad what he thinks.

A muscle twitches in his neck. After a few moments a little grunting noise escapes from his throat. I have never seen him display this amount of emotion, and I feel a sudden lurching pain in the centre of my chest.

He bites his lip. His breathing is fast and shallow. His nostrils dilate.

"She wanted that little house in Brighton so badly, didn't she?" I whisper, hating myself for bringing it up but unable to stop.

"She would have had it too," he blurts out, leaping from his chair and going towards the small drinks fridge in the corner of the dining room. He snaps open a bottle of Star beer, wipes the top with his hand and tilts the bottle to his lips. "I've been saving up for it … for years. *Years!* Working all hours."

I can't believe what I'm hearing. He has always said that Ghana is our home and why does anybody want to live in England, with all those high prices and that miserable weather. He sees the look of disbelief on my face and nods. There is even a slight smile that softens the usual firm set of his jaw as though he can sense my empathy. Almost a smile of achievement, I think, yet I know it can't be because he is the most modest man I have ever known; a man who always refuses to acknowledge any degree of success.

But he has opened up. I can hardly believe that he has opened up and I suspect I haven't heard it all yet.

"On one of my UK breaks," he says, staring at the bubbles rising up the neck of the beer bottle, "I asked an estate agent to look out for something suitable –"

"And?"

He shakes his head. "After Gillian's first operation I told them to forget it." His voice is choked.

"Dad … why?" I feel like hitting him. "She would have loved it – even if it was only for a little while." I bite my lip to stop the sudden quiver at the thought of what my words mean.

"You don't understand, Nikki. By then I needed the money for …" he takes a long slow breath "… for something else."

"Something else? What else could be more important, Dad?"

"Nikki, your mother will hear you. You know how arguing upsets her."

"Dad, I'm not arguing." I lower my voice. "I just think you could have done this one thing for her."

I look at him with growing exasperation. Why is he so damned uncommunicative? My mother is just the same. I adore them both but oh, if only they would share more with each other. And with me. I feel so alone sometimes, almost as though I'm a visitor in the house. I'm getting nowhere with my father, and by the look on his face it's obvious he is not going to open up any more.

"Maybe we should both go to bed," I reluctantly suggest. "You must be tired."

He still says nothing but I have the feeling that those intense blue eyes are almost willing me to stay up with him. I raise my eyebrows, giving him one more chance. Then I walk away, certain that in the few seconds before I turn my back, he seems to be reaching out to me.

* * *

Like clockwork cuckoos, the bulbuls in the tree outside my window spring out from their leafy beds and wake me just before six. Heralding the dusty, misty dawn with their songs of self-adulation, they seem to add an extra trill of happiness at the end of each 'I'm a Pretty Bird' chorus.

I watch at eye-level the songbirds flit from one branch to another. Please let Adam get the gold, I say to the rhythm of the songs, over and over again until the words lull me into a kind of semi-trance. But it's too hot to lie in bed, and quickly I throw off the sheet.

I stand at the window, breathing in the sweet smell of jasmine as the smoke from distant fires snakes into the dawn air. As I look down across the hills and valleys, the galampsays still beating out their steady cacophony of percussion, I'm reminded of how sleep had evaded me until the early hours of the morning. What would Adam's message say, I had wondered, over and over again. Would we succeed in getting the gold? And then what? Would the Kondahene sell us the precious plants? Or would he be too high and mighty on his stool of gold in his remote, protected kingdom? He is not just any ordinary being. He is a powerful, important tribal chief. A king. Would I be able to penetrate the barrier such a man wraps around himself?

Soon the early morning sounds of Dad splashing in the shower and Joseph clattering in the kitchen penetrate my reverie. I slip a thin shapeless cotton dress over my head, then creep up to Mum's room. The door is open. I stand quite still for a few moments, watching her, listening to her laboured breathing. She is a deathly white colour and I have a sudden vision of her with rosy cheeks and a smile on her face as she responds to the Kondahene's wonder plant –

I close my eyes and the vision fades into the white walls of the bedroom, like the fade-out in one of those films where they don't want you to see the horror to come, but only to imagine it.

When I reach the dining room Dad is already eating his slice of pawpaw.

"May I have the car tomorrow, please Dad?" I boldly ask, for there is no other way to do it.

His newly shaven face is smooth, without any expression. "Not Kotonka again, I hope. The shock absorbers won't take many more trips on that road."

"No. Not Kotonka. I just want to have a look around Tarkwa town. Buy some cotton prints. Have a manicure –"

"You! A manicure? In Tarkwa!"

Dad's normally unresponsive face breaks into a pattern of creases like the lines on the batiks Mum buys from Ali to adorn our plain white walls, exchanging the batiks at the back door for clothes I've grown out of.

But in a moment his handsome face is

smooth again, although his eyes have a guilty look, perhaps at having shown such unaccustomed humour.

"I don't know what's so funny," I say. "It'll be much cheaper than in London."

* * *

Today is passing as though it has forty-eight hours. Sweat trickles down my legs in itchy rivulets as the humidity continues to rise. My endless glasses of orange juice leave puddles of condensation on Mum's precious polished mahogany table. The cicadas drone and the crows strut around outside the kitchen door waiting for the daily pickings from Joseph's waste bin.

I spend as much time with my mother as I can, but after another sleepless night I'm in a state of exhaustion – exacerbated by a fever of expectation that I dare not even try to put into words in case they evaporate like the early morning mist that swirls through the valleys and over the tops of the hills before you can count to ten.

* * *

At last the moment arrives. David drives me to the Jesus Lives Beauty Salon. At precisely twelve noon I push aside the starched net curtain.

A young woman, her voluptuous curved body stylishly swathed in a purple print dress with huge puffed sleeves and high matching turban, steps forward to greet me. "You are welcome," she says with a radiant smile.

"Rosie?"

She extends a cool hand. "How are you?" she says.

"I'm fine. How are you? I've come for a manicure."

She escorts me to a wooden chair painted in a shiny metallic pink. It is in a fully reclined position. "Please, relax," she orders.

For the next three-quarters of an hour I almost forget the purpose of my visit as I enjoy my first ever professional manicure. I am fascinated by Rosie's beauty and grace – a perfect advert for her business. And she certainly knows her business.

But of the vital piece of paper Adam promised, there is not a single sign.

I carefully watch her face, looking for some cryptic sign she may be saving until she can see I am at bursting point to know what it is that she has to reveal to me. But there is nothing but this Mona Lisa smile she somehow manages to keep imprinted on her face without any other sign of emotion.

I stand up. I pretend to admire my dazzling nails but can hardly contain myself as I wait for something to happen.

What if it's all a mistake? Perhaps Adam failed to make contact. Perhaps he failed to find any galampsays willing to part with enough gold, even with the promise of the eventual generous reward.

Rosie smiles sweetly. Almost too sweetly.

Oh, no! Surely it can't go wrong now. I can't ask her outright because I might unwittingly say the wrong thing. My heart beats thump-thump in my chest, faster and faster as the seconds tick by. I pay the three hundred *cedis*, convinced the mission has reached an impasse. I try not to tell myself that after I walk out of the Jesus Lives Beauty Salon there will be no way of Adam contacting me, and no way of me tracing him. Oh my God! It will be the end of the trail!

As I turn to go, Rosie gives me another of her radiant smiles. "Would you like a receipt?" she asks.

"Well, yes ... I ... yes please," I say, mainly to delay the feeling of total failure which is beginning to creep over me with the inevitability of a flow of lava from an erupting volcano that will obliterate all hope and all life.

With a chewed yellow biro pen, Rosie laboriously writes the word 'manicure' and adds the figure of three hundred in the right hand column. It is as though she is enjoying inflicting a slow process of torture on me.

Finally she tears out the flimsy page. By this time I can hardly breathe. Then almost as an afterthought she scribbles something else on the bottom line, quickly folds the receipt and hands it to me.

"Thank you," I manage to say, hardly daring to hope that the final words she has written will contain some kind of message.

David opens the car door. I settle myself on the front seat, my head swimming as we swerve and bucket along the pot-holed Tarkwa roads. I keep my eyes straight ahead, afraid to open the piece of paper in front of David.

I am hardly out of the car before I'm running into the house. Mum is asleep so I flee to the bathroom. With trembling hands I open the piece of paper.

'Busua Beach. Eleven-thirty tomorrow'.
Nothing more.

After such a build-up it's almost an anti-climax. This is it, then. Tomorrow at Busua Beach somebody, somehow, is going to hand over the gold to me, which I will then take to the Kondahene from whom I will receive the miracle plants. Adam must have succeeded in persuading the galampsays that they would be handsomely paid for their gold – far more than they would get from the local sharks – once he convinces the pharmaceutical company of the vital necessity of acquiring these plants with the unique qualities we are certain will transform the treatment of breast cancer and other vicious cancers.

It feels as though someone has thrown a bucket of ice cold water over me, revitalising every cell in my body.

I stare at the piece of paper wondering why Adam hasn't told me more.

Where on Busua Beach am I to meet this

person? Or persons? Man or woman?

How and when will I travel to the Kondahene?

And what should I do with the plants when I get them? Will Adam be there to give them the special protection they will need when they leave the sanctuary of the rain forest?

The questions buzz around my head, not least of all the problem of yet again asking Dad for the car. But I console myself with the thought that I can go on a mammy-wagon if the worst comes to the worst. The wooden seats are hard, and there are no shock absorbers, but none of this matters if it gets you where you need to be.

* * *

"I'm dying to go to the beach, Dad," I say when he comes home at his usual late hour. "I've only been once this holiday and I'll get back to England with no tan and nobody will believe

I've been to Africa."

A strange expression crosses Dad's face, one that I haven't ever seen before, and for a moment my hopes sink.

"Why don't you take the car tomorrow?" he says, looking straight into my eyes. "I'll tell David to pick you up as soon as he's dropped me at Kwame." His voice is pitched to a level which takes it out of the usual monotonous, disinterested timbre and I can't believe how accommodating he is being. Perhaps he is suffering feelings of guilt? Maybe he realises I could do with a bit of fun now and then. His generous offer almost makes me forget the serious nature of my journey. I adore the beach. Yes. I never miss an opportunity to go. Yes. But these sentiments are going to take second place to tomorrow's momentous events.

"By the way, don't disturb Gillian before you go," he says. "I've managed to persuade her to have one of those really strong pain killers Dr

Tufor gave her yesterday. It's a strong dose of morphine, I believe. She should sleep tonight and most of the day tomorrow. We'll leave her in bed instead of carrying her to the chair. Joseph will watch her carefully and give her another one if she appears restless or in pain."

"Thank goodness for that," I murmur softly to myself, my feelings of guilt slightly appeased, and grateful that our Gillian will have some respite from the pain.

Dad picks up his briefcase. "I'm off to bed. Enjoy yourself tomorrow."

"Thanks, Dad." I take a step towards him. He seems to hesitate. Perhaps he's waiting for me to kiss him, but before I can he turns and walks out.

* * *

Tossing and turning between the damp sheets, I ponder over what I will carry the gold in. Will my blue canvas bag be large enough? I have no idea how much gold we are borrowing, how heavy it will be, or how light.

In the morning I peep into Mum's bedroom to see her still fast asleep, a misleadingly serene look on the pale, drawn features. The devoted Joseph has already brought a fresh flask of water and removed yesterday's clothes for laundering. Her sheet has also been straightened. I lean over and gently kiss her forehead. She does not move. A pang of fear shoots through me. Should I be leaving her?

* * *

I sit on the veranda waiting for David to arrive. I look down into the valley. The clanking noises seem louder than usual, but thank goodness Mum won't hear them. The mist is thick and the air humid, enveloping me with its cloying heat, wafting the heavy scent of jasmine into my nostrils. A vulture sits in the Pretty Birds' tree, silencing them with his menacing pose of superiority as he glares hunchbacked into the steaming valley.

At David's first hoot I am through the door. I sit tensely next to him, trying to psyche myself up for the task in front of me.

I hardly see the deep green shadows of the jungle, the swamps with their myriad bamboos, long and thick and yellow. I hardly notice the women with their Singer sewing machines on their heads and the laughing, waving children, nor the vultures circling the piles of rotting goodness-knows-what, and the goats wandering across the road in their singularly stupid manner.

Then vaguely I register the regimented rows of rubber trees that flash by mile after mile, telling me we are getting closer to the port of Takoradi where David will turn off towards Busua Beach.

I wonder if it is all a dream.

Suddenly rows of dead, leafless, disease-stricken palm trees come into view, standing like petrified soldiers at the end of a battle, and then we are driving through the little village of Busua.

I smell the fresh salty sea air. In my mind's eye I can already see the relentless rollers roaring onto the long sandy beach. I feel the same excitement I always feel when I'm approaching the mighty Atlantic Ocean with its mountainous waves sparkling like diamonds in the sun. Only this time it is intensified by the flow of adrenaline flooding my veins at the thought of what is about to happen.

* * *

David stops the car in the usual place opposite the dilapidated beach shelters. Treasure Island, as I have always called it, stands out in all its tropical unreality on the horizon, its two giant palm trees piercing the cerulean blue of the sky.

I glance at my watch. I'm half an hour early, so there's time for a swim. If I don't swim, David will wonder why. While he takes my old wooden surf-board from the car boot, I slide out of my matching blouse and shorts, glad that I'd put my swim suit on under my clothes.

Clutching the board I run across the golden sand towards the thundering waves that lace the beach for a mile and a half both east and west of the shelters.

For a few minutes I let the tepid water wash over my body, revelling in its refreshing silkiness. Then I wade through the foaming waves and turn, positioning the board to catch a whopper that sweeps me all the way back to the beach. Over and over again I throw myself into the waves, carefully yet instinctively timing their moment of maximum force, going further out each time, though wary of the treacherous undertow so unpredictable on this wild westerly coast of Africa.

At the end of a really good run I am sitting in

the shallow hissing water regaining my breath, wiping my eyes, when something makes me look up.

Until now the beach has been empty, except for a few women walking towards Dixcove with top-heavy bundles of sticks on their heads. But now, suddenly, there is a man standing on the beach, fully dressed, looking out to sea.

I narrow my eyes in case I'm mistaken.

But I am not.

It is unmistakably my father.

I panic.

What is he doing here?

Oh no! This will ruin everything. He never comes to the beach with me. On any other day I would be thrilled to see him. But today ... oh no! But how did he get here? I have his car.

Quickly I look up and down the beach, hoping to see whoever it is I'm supposed to meet, and warn them not to approach me yet. It must be almost eleven-thirty. Damn, he couldn't have timed his fatherly visit at a worse moment.

Then my anger softens and a lump fills my throat. Perhaps he was on his way to a meeting in Accra in a company car and decided to stop for a few minutes to see me. It would be a first and here I am, cursing him.

As I walk towards him he begins to move across the beach towards me.

We walk at the same slow pace, still uncertain, still unbelieving, our eyes riveted to each other's eyes.

He stops at a distance of about ten yards.

I stop too.

"Nikki?" he says.

"What is it, Dad? You look as though you've seen a ghost."

He gives no answer, but goes on looking at me.

"What's wrong? Why are you here?" I ask. And then in a sudden flash of terror I am certain I know.

I run towards him. "Is it Mum? Oh, no,

please don't tell me it's Mum —"

I grip both his arms, digging my fingers frantically into his flesh. But he holds himself rigid, not responding to me in any way.

I can't stand it. All I can think of is that even at such a terrible moment he has no feeling. He's inhuman. He's cold. He has no love in him.

I turn away to hide my tears, burying my face in my sandy hands.

Disregarding my obvious distress, he speaks at last.

"Do you know Adam Afari?"

I spin round and look at him with horror.

"Adam?"

His eyes blaze but he does not answer me.

I hug my arms and bite my lip. I glance at Dad's wrist watch. It is exactly eleven-thirty. Then I spot the old battered briefcase, sitting on the beach close to his feet.

Is it him?

It can't be.

Is he the one who is going to supply us with the gold?

But this is impossible.

My own father!

How?

"Yes, I know Adam," I say, my eyes filling with tears, unable to cope with the double knowledge that floods my being with waves of disbelief.

Is he human after all?

And then, suddenly, from knowing nothing about my father, I feel as though I know everything.

At this exact moment he reaches out and takes me in his arms. Holding my wet, sticky, sandy body close to his chest, he rocks me to and fro. We do not need to speak.

It is enough that we are both here, standing in the middle of the beach at exactly eleven-thirty, with the roar of the sea pounding in our ears.

It tells us both everything we need to know.

Except for the burning question of where he got the gold.

It flashes through my mind how almost over-willing he was last night to let me have his car – no doubt not wanting to let on how badly he himself needed it at exactly the same time and the same day at Busua Beach. No doubt needing to hide his own need.

With an urgency Dad seldom shows, he picks up the black briefcase and leads me to the car. He holds the car door open for me.

"Let's go to the little beach bar where we can talk," he says, after I had wriggled out of my wet sandy costume and into my clothes, all the time trying to fathom from the depths of my psyche what all this can possibly mean.

"How did you get here, Dad?" I ask as we settle down on the back seat, David already at the wheel.

He laughs. "Shh! Never mind. But it wasn't the most comfortable journey I've ever had!"

"You didn't want me to think you were doing

anything unusual!" I whisper, echoing his laughter.

In the heat of the grubby beach bar we hold hands – the first time we have ever done this – while I tell him how I had met Adam on the plane and been totally won over by his passionate plan to capture one of Africa's ancient natural remedies and persuade the pharmaceutical company to present it to the world in order to try to cure the millions of cancer patients, some with little hope of recovery.

"I wanted so badly to do something to help Mum. When you said there was nothing more they could do, I couldn't bear the thought of her dying. But of course when I got home and saw her I realised our plan might be ... might be too late for her ... but by then I couldn't stop – because there were others ..."

Dad takes a clean neatly folded white handkerchief from his pocket and hands it to me. He waits for me to dry my eyes, then urges me to tell him the whole story.

"Adam really opened my eyes, Dad. He told me how the giant drug companies are vying with each other, exploiting nature's vast array of natural resources. But because they're governed by the shareholders' need for a steady and ever-increasing profit, they aren't always willing to make the rewards sufficiently attractive to the custodians of some of the world's most ancient natural remedies."

Dad nods and takes a long, deep breath, as though what he is planning to say next is taxing his every belief. "We live in a capitalist world, Nikki. The arrangement has to be mutually beneficial." He pats the black briefcase at his feet but does not look at me.

"Did Adam tell you he grew up in a village on the edge of the rain forest?" Dad nods, but I still feel compelled to carry on. "He says he knows that this plant, if combined with other specially synthesised drugs, would target certain cancers. And would have the capacity to kill certain cells, and not others. And that it would be one of the biggest breakthroughs in medical history today."

"He convinced me too, and that's why I'm here."

"Oh, Dad. Aren't we lucky that this little patch of rain forest has so far managed to survive."

"Only because the Kondahene guards it with his life." He pours more of the now lukewarm beer into our glasses.

There is an awkward pause as we almost revert to our former distant shyness, as though our newly found discovery of each other is too much to comprehend.

At last he says, "Nikki?"

"Yes, Dad ..."

"You do realise, don't you, that it could be years before results of laboratory tests lead to the commercial synthesisation by the chemists. And by then –"

"Yes, I know that now. But Dad, how long have you –"

"Had the gold?" His laugh is brittle. He looks at me as though he is seeking my help for the right words, yet hoping I won't need a full explanation. He probably can't even formulate it in his own mind, I think, let alone explain it to this girl, this daughter of his who has been a stranger to him for so long. But now that the gold has opened the door between us he surely knows he will have to tell me.

"Not long," he says at last. "Ever since the doctors told me there was nothing more they could do and I knew I had to do something myself to save Gillian. It hasn't been easy to buy it. But I would have done anything. Anything –"

I put my arms around him. He bends his head towards me as though this is the first time in many years that he has found solace in another person's arms, and he can hardly believe it.

I hold him closer.

"You see, Nikki dear, I realised that … that I

couldn't live without her. When I heard whispers about the plant and its amazing properties, and that the Kondahene would only take gold in payment, I began in a frenzy buying it from the galampsays, using the money I'd saved up for the little house in Brighton and working all hours to make more, though I had no idea what I'd do with the plant if I ever managed to get it. I'd worked so hard to save all that money. And then, when I knew she wouldn't make it ... well, I couldn't undo what I'd already done, and though I was still working in the dark, as it were, I became obsessed with the thought of all the people in the world who would benefit." He screws up his eyes tightly. "Even though it was too late for Gillian."

A tear escapes and trickles down his cheek.

I reach for his hand. And it suddenly hits me that the money he has worked so hard to earn he is now giving freely and without reservation to the Kondahene in order to help save the lives of cancer sufferers all over the world.

What a man!

"Oh, Nikki, if only she'd told me about the early symptoms, maybe it —"

"Don't torture yourself, Dad." I grasp his other hand. "How could you have known?"

A little black girl with wide searching eyes and plaits sticking up all over her head like a porcupine and a broad sympathetic smile lighting up her face brings another two bottles of Star beer, as though she knows we need them. She pours some frothily into each of the empty glasses.

Dad brushes away a persistent fly and takes a sip of his beer. "The thing is, Nikki, I *did* know that something was wrong." He turns his head away. "But not what to do about it."

"But you never asked her, did you? Oh, Dad." I grasp his shoulders and turn him back to face me. "Don't feel so bad. It takes two people to lose touch with each other. It was just as much her fault as yours, with her stoic upbringing, ignoring the pain, and her determination never to let you down by making you think she was unhappy."

He puts his elbows on the table and grips the sides of his face. Then he looks at me as though suddenly making up his mind.

"I started out blindly. Even if I'd known what to do I couldn't have done it on my own. I had bought all that gold but I didn't know how to go about it. And then when things didn't seem to be working out I even thought again about the little house in Brighton. Some happiness for her last few months. But I knew she wouldn't leave now so I just carried on, waiting, hoping –"

"And then Adam came along."

He takes a long gulp of his beer. "And so did you, Nikki." He shakes his head but doesn't say what is clearly in his mind, that this is a coincidence he could not have dreamt of. "Come on, we have things to do, you and I. Finish your beer."

* * *

I can see that David is puzzled at the turn of events. Normally he would have had the radio on all the way from Busua Beach to Tarkwa to drown the silence in the back seat of the car. But now he turns it off, obviously trying to catch some of the non-stop conversation coming from his usually uncommunicative employer and his daughter. But we keep our unaccustomed chatter so low that he can't possibly hear enough to piece together anything substantial.

As we approach our house I imagine Mum hearing the car coming up the hill and easing her aching body into an upright position, making sure she doesn't let anybody see that she's been lying in bed all day.

We pull up at the front door. Dad puts two hundred cedis dash into David's hand and asks him to report back tomorrow morning at six-thirty to take me on a long journey.

Surprisingly, he also tells him when and where to find Adam, who will be anxiously waiting to carry out the next step in transporting the precious cargo to Europe – that is, if I succeed in getting the Kondahene to be part of our plan.

"Yes, Mr. Parker," David answers, clearly frustrated that he is not even being told yet where I am going.

* * *

I feel strongly that Dad and I should show Mum as soon as we arrive home that something important has happened; that a new era has been borne out of our joint need to help the most important person in both our lives. Clearly Dad thinks the same, for without saying a word he takes my hand and we walk into Mum's room together.

In spite of her semi-comatose state her eyes widen with amazement. She looks even more surprised to see that we are holding hands, and knowing Mum she must be wondering why we're glancing at each other as though there is some sort of conspiracy going on between us. She is probably afraid that we've been planning to get her moved to the hospital and she's already made up her mind she isn't going. Open mouthed, her shoulders hunched, she waits for an explanation.

Dad and I sit down on either side of the bed. She looks first at Dad and then at me, visibly puzzled by our expressions. She knows us too well not to be able to see the uncertainty and the guilt, but the exultation too that exudes from our faces.

I can read her thought processes as though she is saying them out loud. *I have never known them to share a secret before. But if they have a secret it is certainly none of my business to ask about it.*

And so she waits patiently.

"We've something to tell you, Mum. Why don't you get into a more comfortable position.

Dad, please fetch Mum another pillow."

She watches wide-eyed as Brad does as I request.

And for the next hour as our story unfolds, her mouth stays open as though she can't believe what she is hearing.

At first it is shock, but when Dad tells her he'd initially saved the money for the little house, a rare glow spreads across her face as if this miracle has actually happened, as if knowing it was a possibility is enough to make her dream come true. And I have a sudden poignant vision of the sun rising over the sea at Brighton and enveloping her in its wintry warmth.

When it is clear that we have finished our story, she takes our hands in each of hers, shaking her head at the wonder of it all.

It is a breathtakingly beautiful moment, without words, but laden with more emotion than has ever passed between the three of us before.

Outside, the galampsays are pounding and clattering in a frenzy of gold extraction.

A crow squawks and a bulbul says, "I'm a Pretty bird."

And Mum says, quietly, looking at each of us in turn, "Oh, I am so happy. And so proud."

She smiles, sinks back on her pillows and slowly closes her eyes.

* * *

I sit on the veranda and relive every moment of the last two sensational weeks. I peep in every half hour at Mum. Dad is at the mine and Mum has just had one of Dr Tufor's knock-out Morphine pills he says she must have from now on, which keep her out of pain, asleep most of the time, and far calmer than usual when she is awake.

It could happen at any moment now, Dr Tufor told Dad and me the last time we spoke to him.

Just once when she senses my presence, she opens her eyes, looks at a vulture sitting on a branch outside the window and says: "Vulture is an ugly word, isn't it, Nikki dear." Then her face softens. "But look at him! The word does not suit him. He's really quite beautiful, you know. And he helps to keep Ghana clean, doesn't he, Nikki dear."

I smile at her, hiding my tears. And then she is asleep again. I bend down and gently press my cheek to hers. I stay there as long as I can. As I kiss her forehead her eyelids flicker. I hold her hand, so soft in mine.

At that moment I hear Dad's car crunching up the hill. It stops with a screech of breaks and a banging door. Then loud footsteps march into the house.

I meet him half way down the passage. His face is set and drawn

"Dad? What's wrong? Why are you home?" Normally he never comes home during a working day. He never has before.

He stops for a moment "I've taken two weeks' leave. To be with Gillian."

* * *

I resume my seat on the veranda. My suitcase is packed. Tears stream down my cheeks as they seem to have done most of the day, and my mind leaps back to my breathtakingly exciting journey north to one of the most beautiful unspoilt areas of this wonderful country; to an experience I could never have dreamt could have been more beautiful.

It seems we are expected, for no sooner has our car approached than we are surrounded by a welcoming party, all dressed in brightly coloured traditional dress and all smiling. I am thankful that Dad suggested I wear my best Kente cloth *caba*, and made sure my sandals are highly polished.

I am led to a rough building with a steep thatched roof, the walls the colour of the red earth. A central courtyard is just beyond my vision, its white walls highly decorated with bold designs in red, black, green and yellow.

The light is dim, but I can just make out a figure about ten yards away, seated on an ornately decorated stool, the gold insets gleaming in the faint light.

I walk slowly towards him, aware of an aura of saintliness I have never felt in anyone before. Although the face I see is sinewy and creased, the eyes are soft and wide open, and I know that I am in the presence of someone who is almost spiritual.

I approach just short of where he is seated.

I stop.

I bow slightly.

Just as I am prepared to kneel in front of him, he rises to his feet to greet me, extending his hand. This is most unusual, as it is I, as the visitor, who should make the first greeting.

I move forward and take it – a firm hand devoid of any flabbiness, despite his advanced age. I ask him how he is. "*Wo ho te sane?*" I say in what I hope is my best Twi.

"*Me ho ye*," he says, the normal response to indicate he is fine.

I hold my breath. With my right hand I dig into my blue canvas bag. I take a deep breath. This is the moment of truth.

I take out the thirty-five ozs of gold, not in one polished nugget that would be the ideal, but in many small rough edged pieces, which seem to delight him as I hand them to him one by one. His mouth opens and he takes a long, deep breath. From the courtyard beyond us comes the sound of drumming and singing that starts softly and gradually increases until it penetrates every atom of my body with its intensity.

As suddenly as it started, it stops.

I breathe in deeply.

The tension is palpable. What will happen

next? Where are the precious plants?

The Kondahene finally moves towards me. From a small ornate table next to him, he hands me the precious plants, wrapped in layers of leaves and smelling of a mixture of every fresh herb Joseph has ever used in our kitchen.

In a trance I take them from him. Someone behind me appears with a tray covered in even more moisture laden leaves and invites me to place the precious parcel in the tray.

The night that follows is filled with more drumming, singing, dancing and prayer, that carries on till midnight. While this is going on, the Kondahene chats to me in perfect English, and it warms my heart to realise how many ideas we have in common.

Early the following morning the Kondahene bids me a fond farewell as though we have known each other all our lives. He could not have been more charming to me or more willing to help, grateful to receive the gold which he says he will use to continue to protect the forest.

Before sunrise David and I are on our way. About half an hour after leaving, David stops the car on the outskirts of a small village. He opens the door for me and I get out. He does not speak but at the edge of my vision I see Adam. He walks slowly towards us and kneels beside me. He too is in traditional dress.

I hand the parcel to Adam, who with his head still bowed disappears as silently as he had appeared, into the mists behind me.

And he is now on his way with the precious plants safely protected to keep them alive until they reach their final destination.

We will meet again one day soon – Adam and me. And Dad. To make more plans if this one succeeds.

Yes, the future is still uncertain, but as I sit here on the veranda, waiting for David to take me to the airport, soaking up the sounds of bamboo leaves shivering and palm fronds clattering and bees buzzing busily around brilliant red hibiscus and pink frangipanis; of drums beating and hooters hooting, cocks crowing and crows squawking, crickets screeching and bulbuls telling each other, 'I'm a pretty bird,' and drifting up from the lush green valleys the sound of people laughing and talking and singing and playing music, I know what it is, for the first time in my life – no matter what the final outcome is – exactly what Adam had meant by *a sense of fulfilment*.

Author's Note

Although inspired by a real situation, this is a work of fiction. The events described are imaginary and the characters are fictitious. It is not intended that any reader infer that these incidents are real or that the events actually happened.

I apologise for taking certain liberties in the naming of two fictitious gold mines in Ghana and one fictitious mining town. I have also invented a fictitious tribal king – a leader of a fictitious kingdom of the Ghananian people.

However, everything else in this story is factual.

The plundering of the forests continues.

THE END

Coming Soon ...

Sheila Mary Taylor's

forthcoming romantic legal thriller,

set in Cape Town, South Africa

SILENT JUSTICE

Chapter 1

November 2014

Tanya

I'm really lucky that I am still able to write. Well, tap the keys would be a more accurate way of describing the laborious way I now have of communicating.

You see, theoretically I'm paralysed from the neck down, but only I know, and Victoria knows, that actually I am now only paralysed from the waist down. Well, half and half. I don't know the medical term for it, and I can't describe the strange half-and-half state my body is in. Because although my right arm is still completely useless, parts of my left hand now just manage to move.

One finger, in fact.

At first I thought I was imagining that I could move it. The feeling of elation threatened to take my breath clean away, and I soon persuaded myself that I had been in a kind of semi-comatose state when I thought I had seen one finger of my left hand moving.

But one day soon after that, as I sat drinking in the sounds of the sea and the snorting of the horses, and breathing in the smell of the fynbos and the stables and the grass, there was no denying that there was movement.

What an incredible feeling it was.

It wasn't the whole hand, but just that one finger.

The second time I saw it, it happened like this:

Victoria pushes me along the winding path to the shade of the oak trees that cluster on the crest of the craggy hill behind the Old Cape homestead. The wheels crush the acorns. Birds flutter to safety and beetles scurry to the undisturbed undergrowth beneath the gnarled trees lining the daily route to my favourite place on earth.

I gaze at the deep blue sea stretching over the curve of the earth for thousands of miles to the Antarctic, and I marvel that I can sit contentedly for hours, smelling the pungent salty air and thinking about the wonderful life I have led … even though every day I ask myself –

Why did it all end? Was it all my fault? What can I do about it now and how can I do it quickly enough before the court case ends and the verdict is announced?

How can I ensure that justice is done?

How?

I think about what I had in abundance for such a short glorious time; but inevitably I cringe when I think about what happened to end it all ...

At first I was reluctant to even let these soul-crunching thoughts pass through my mind. For months I held them at bay. I erected a steel wall in my mind because it was too painful to let even one stray thought wriggle into my mind to cause an avalanche of memories ...

As Victoria and I are sitting gazing out across the sea – as we are wont to do in complete harmony – something makes me look down at my hand and at the same time Victoria looks at it too, then quickly looks away. But just as quickly we both look at my hand again.

The finger moves. The middle one. Jerkily at first. And hardly discernible.

At last Victoria looks into my eyes.

'Tanya,' she says.

'Yes, Victoria.'

'There is enough movement in that finger … just enough movement to strike the gentle keys of a laptop.'

I smile at her and turn my head away from the finger, back to the vista of the sea spread out before us. I think what a wonderful woman she is, always so full of hope. But I say nothing.

I haven't told Father or Anton or Lizette that I can use my left hand. And I'm sure Victoria has not told them either. They would immediately haul me off to Constantiaberg Hospital for tests. And I never want to see the inside of that place again. I often overhear them talking about the "miracle" all three of them are still hoping might happen to their poor darling Tanya. I'm sure the doctors were only trying to soften the blow when they said there was a faint chance I would gradually regain the use of my limbs.

You see, apart from my one clever writing finger, I don't ever want that to happen.

I don't want to walk.

I don't want to be made to look normal.

I don't ever want to be confronted with having to explain to my friends what happened to disfigure me.

With a face as twisted and mutilated as mine, I would never want to show it to the special friends I once had. That would not be fair to them. They should be allowed to remember me as I was. I couldn't bear it if they pitied me.

    I'm perfectly happy the way I am, safe in my own little world, being looked after by the kindest, wisest, most special woman I have ever known – second only to my poor dead mother.

The day Victoria brings me the little laptop she's been frantically saving up to buy, she tells me she thinks writing more of the poems she always loved to hear me recite to her when I was still able to speak, would be one way of purging whatever feelings of hatred I harboured within my broken body.

    But I have other ideas.

    And it is only when I begin to write it all down that I find myself fascinated by the way the web of events was woven, without ever realising at the time what tragedy it was presaging.

So beautiful are some of these thoughts, yet so cruel and so evil are others, it is almost as though they were pre-ordained by some invisible hand that was as much mixed up by the complexities of the people involved as the complexities of this beautiful land we live in.

Now that I have started to write down the events I realise how vital it is for me to record it all as quickly as possible.

For even as convoluted as they are, time is short and I must hurry.

The court case is already under way. It is shown on TV every day although I never watch it and as far as I know no-one else in our household is allowed to watch it either.

But my telling of it is painfully slow. Each day – up here in my favourite secret place – I struggle to get the words down, not only because I can only write one or two words a minute, but because it is essential that every word must be the truth.

So it takes a great deal of thinking, searching and remembering. Not only must I search my mind to know what to tell, but I must search my mind about what *not* to tell.

For the truth to be meaningful – and relevant to the court case – not every happening has to be revealed. Nor would I want all those exquisite details to be revealed to the scandal-loving *Cape Argus* and *Cape Times* editorial vultures who would not think twice about splashing the secrets of the most beautiful love affair – the only love affair I ever had – to their vapid undiscerning readers.

Court cases are sometimes painfully slow, but I cannot rely on this case going on indefinitely. For justice to be done, I have to get this confession as soon as possible into the hands of those who are going to be able to turn things around.

'*Ya, my skat,*' she says in a rare lapse into her mother tongue, 'if you can do anything now, it will ensure that justice will be done.'

Even though physical love is now denied me, having experienced the most exquisite love any woman could possibly have is enough to keep me going for the rest of my life.

Yes, I think, stroking my swollen belly as I do every day, hardly able to wait for the first signs of movement. I have a great deal to live for, and if I am lucky, to see justice done.

But I must hurry. The court case will soon end and every second counts.

Printed in Great Britain
by Amazon